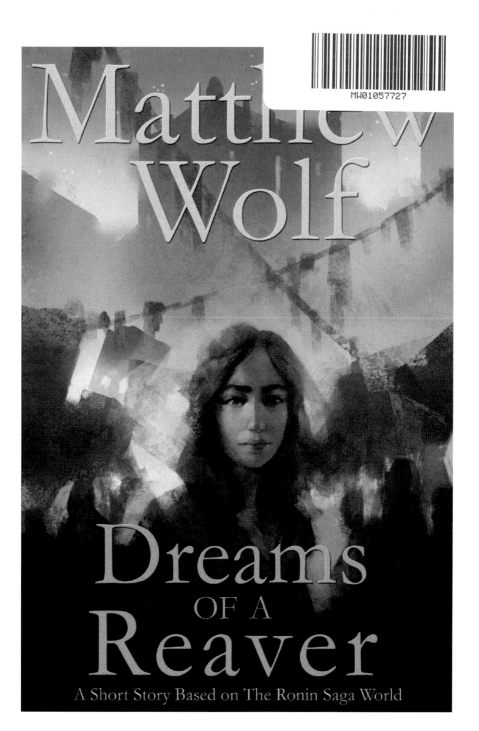

Matthew Wolf

Dreams
OF A
Reaver

A Short Story Based on The Ronin Saga World

DREAMS OF A REAVER

A Short Story Based on the Ronin Saga World

Matthew Wolf

Copyright © 2014 by Matthew Wolf. All rights reserved.

This book is a work of fiction. Names, characters, places and incidents are either products of the author's imagination or used fictitiously. Any resemblance to actual events, locales, or persons, living or dead, is entirely coincidental. All rights reserved. No part of this publication can be reproduced or transmitted in any form or by any means, electronic or mechanical, without permission from the author.

eBook designed by MC Writing

DREAMS OF A REAVER

A Short Story Based on the Ronin Saga World

MATTHEW WOLF

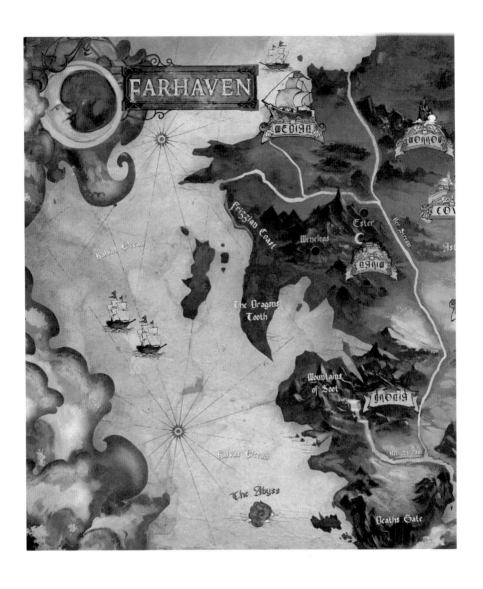

Dreams of a Reaver

HAWKERS AND MERCHANTS CRIED OUT AS Miriam left a wave of dust in her wake, but she paid them little heed as she pressed through the crowded desert streets, moving with purpose.

Today, her dreams would come true.

The marketplace was always chaotic. A hum of voices, from gossiping merchants to loud-mouthed hawkers, to the glaring sun high above that baked the bone-dry air—Farbs was a world always in motion. But there was something else. She felt it in the air—like the charged hum before a coming storm. It made her skin prickle and the hairs on her arms stood on end.

A change was coming...

A change meant an end. An end to the dreaded tannery that each day left her skin smelling more of putrid sulfur, a stink she couldn't wash out no matter how much soap she used or how hard she scrubbed. And yet her heart fluttered at that thought. She was scared to leave the only thing she knew. And more importantly, how would she help provide for her family? Life in Farbs was hard for those with work... But without? She nearly shivered despite the heat. Still, change also meant a beginning. Miriam smiled at last, welcoming the hum of change.

Nimbly, she wove between two fruit sellers apologizing to the men who argued, red-faced, competing for a gaggle of customers. Both colorful carts brimmed with ripe green falquts, and squat brown combersquals. She hesitated as she imagined biting into the sweet, crisp flesh of a juicy falqut. No doubt, it would be perfect on a day such as this to quell the angry heat. But she quickly pushed the temptation away. She had no time for it— *Not today,* she thought with an excited smile.

As she pressed forward, the crowds swarmed around once again, moving like feverish fire ants. Farbs was a city bursting with all manner of people—merchants seeking deals, laborers toiling away, guards with vigilant eyes, dockhands on leave and looking for a drink, and the occasional ruffians scanning for easy prey.

She passed bushels of copper-colored wheat, jugs brimming with dark wines, casks filled with frothing brews, jars and tables piled withherbs of the desert, shining jewelry, and the gloss of fine fabrics. She even saw baskets filled with coiled snakes. She shivered in disgust. It was a delicacy of Farbs, but far from her liking.

Tucked beneath a sky of colorful awnings, the world of the marketplace sat just out of reach of the ferocious orange sun.

Miriam raised her *shaka*, to shield her face from the dust of the city, when suddenly she ran into a wall of flesh. Men and women were packed tighter than a clenched fist.

"What's going on?" she whispered, but received only shrugs in reply.

She maneuvered through the crowd, pushing her way to the front just as an elegant palanquin appeared. It was followed by a host of men and women in scarlet and black cloth. Each danced around the cart, while guards on camels flanked the spectacle. Slowly, they moved beneath the wide arched entryway and into the marketplace proper. Miriam's gaze was glued to the *lecarta*. Its wooden panels were heavily gilded and engraved with the black flame—the Citadel's sigil.

"Who's in there?" she asked.

"Must be someone from the Citadel," replied a woman with her hair piled in a mound upon her head.

"Can't be," said another, "Reavers or Neophytes appearing in this part of town? They wouldn't lower themselves to that. Besides, Reavers aren't ones for fanfare or ceremony."

"You're wrong," Miriam said, watching the procession.

The big man, his thumbs tucked haughtily behind his worn leather vest, stared down at her. He gave an amused snort. "Am I now? And what does a little girl know of dealings with the Citadel?"

Miriam felt the hair on the back of her neck rise. *Little girl?* "A bit more than you it seems. See the curtains of the *lecarta*? They're scarlet, as are the dancers' clothes. It's clearly someone from the Citadel." *But who?* she wondered.

Shirtless men bore the load of the passenger upon their muscled shoulders as they made their way down the wide street where more crowds gathered. The men's skin glistened in the midday sun. The sight of the tan, muscled men wasn't an unpleasant sight in the least, she admitted, feeling her cheeks heat. But her blood burned with thoughts of the Reavers.

Reavers were powerful men and women who wielded the spark and lived within the Citadel, a great keep that overlooked the sprawling metropolis of Farbs. A Reaver was a name uttered with both fear and respect. While the Farbian guards were the peacekeepers of the city, the true power resonated from the Citadel and those within its walls. Reavers were the closest thing Farbs had to kings or queens. They suffered no one. Miriam felt a flush of fear, knowing this... A Reaver wouldn't tolerate a stray hair upon his or her perfect red robes let alone an individual late to their own day of Testing!

"No no no, this can't be! I can't be stuck here, not when they're waiting for me!" She pushed her way forward, but the throng pressed back just as hard. The sweaty mass of bodies felt like a wave of water and she was drowning. She threw herself forward, shouting.

"Calm down, girl," said a big manholding her back.

"Let me go!" she wriggled against his hold. "I need to get through!"

"There's no way you're getting through now. Even if you get through this crowd, those guards will surely throw you back, or, worse yet, into the stockades. You'll have to wait until it's over."

Miriam struggled against the big man as thewoman with the mass of hair upon her head sighed. "Relax, girl. We all have things to do and places to be." She nodded to a nearby cart across the street filled with what looked like decorative ornaments. "See that? I have a shipment of firesparks and sizzlers waiting to be delivered to the Citadel for the grand festival tonight. It is a great honor, but if I don't get them there soon, I'll be out of a good deal of money. We're all stuck here, for now."

Miriam fidgeted, half-listening to the woman. "You don't understand..."

She had waited all her life for this moment. It was the dream of nearly every young girl and boy to be Tested, a dream she thought had died, passing her by when she turned sixteen, but now it was a reality. She was to become a Reaver.She had only to pass the test, one that would determine if she had the spark—the gift of magic. It was a rare opportunity, and unheard of for a girl beyond the age of ten. She knew that, at this very moment, a Reaver was in her home, waiting for her. The thought of a Reaver waiting on her made her palms sweat. If only her mother had not insisted she pick up the Sarien wine to impress their honored guest.

Annoyance ather mother churned like poison in her belly. *Why?* She thought. *Why was her mother such a fool?* All her mother ever cared about was how others viewed her. Bitter memories came rushing back... Her mother wearing her favorite tattered blue silk dress with golden threaded leaves, frayed and drooping from their sleeves—a noble lady's hand-me-down at one time, now it looked ridiculous and sad. It wasn't that she hated her mother for her fancies or her dreams for more—*no,* that she could understand, relate to even—she hated her mother for the unhappiness that had twisted itself inside her, growing into a black pit of bitterness that she directed at all others like a perpetual dark cloud hanging over her and her father.

And now? A stupid bottle of wine to impress her guests would ruin Miriam's dream.

Focus! She told herself, but the world continued to spin. Dust and heat made her dizzy. She felt as if she was being sucked into a whirlpool of flesh. She looked back. Where she came from was lost—just more bodies. Her vision blurred, crowds distorting, as tears sprouted... She felt her dreams collapsing, like a beetle's dry husk getting stepped on. *No!* Her mind shouted. She wouldn't give up that easily. Miriam's eyes snapped open.

I will become a Reaver, she thought.

Delving into her mind, Miriam envisioned an envelope of air surrounding her. She imagined wedging her way through the remaining crowd—those who stood between her and the marching procession. With that image, she closed her eyes to focus and took a step forward. The crush of bodies felt somewhat less thick. Again she pushed, imagining herself as a tiny needle, or an elemental Spryt slipping through the cracks. She felt something flowing around her, the little hairs on her arm rising. Was it wind? No, it was flesh she realized, pricking those that got too close and creating a small window. She smiled in elation, wading deeper through the swamp of people, feeling as if it was thick and syrupy, but each step brought her that much closer... Suddenly she heard the bustle and cries of men and opened her eyes. Before her, a horse reared upon its hind legs, threatening to crush her while the man upon its back wrestled to gain control.

Without thought, Miriam threw the bundle she had been holding, and dove. The wine shattered as she rolled beneath the flailing legs of the beast. The creature stomped down, narrowly missing her. Miriam completed her dive only to be surrounded in a cloud of billowing dust. Coughing, she wiped the sand from her watery eyes. Above her head, she glimpsed wooden slats. The *lecarta*, she realized.Still crouched, she watched as the dust settled. The guards were everywhere. They surrounded her, searching for the intruder. She panicked. There was no way out.

"There she is! Stop right there, criminal!"

As one, the guards advanced. Several drew swords and Miriam flushed in fear, yet she remained still. If they caught her now, at the very least, she would be punished severely. But that was not her main fear. She knew she would not make it home in time. This time, there seemed no escape, no one else to blame but herself, her own limitations. If only she could have the power of a Reaver, then no one would bully her or put her down ever again! But the only sure path ahead was punishment—a hand chopped off for those unruly citizens that defied the Citadel, or *worse*. But the truly worse fate was already clear to Miriam.

She'd never become a Reaver, instead she'd turn bitter and empty, a husk of a human living off the past. Just like her mother.

Miriam closed her eyes in desperation. This time as she delved into her mind she pictured a tiny flame. Yet the spark was nowhere to be seen. *I just used it, didn't I? That had to be the spark!* The shouting of approaching guards grew louder. Her heart thundered in her chest. She clawed for the spark. Still, nothing. Despite her panic, she kept her lids tightly shut. It was the only way her spark ever listened. She pressed harder, and felt a flickering flame in her hands. She poured her fear and need into the flame.

Abruptly, a calloused hand gripped her arm. Miriam reached out, throwing the flame to where she had seen the woman's cart. There was silence as the man tugged at her, and then a loud pop. The ground shuddered. The guard loosened his grip—it was all she needed. Miriam yanked her arm free and leapt towards the crowd as another pop and fizzle rattled the air. There was a ripple of confusion and shuffling as men and women were thrown to their knees. Miriam dove through the slim gap and dashed onward. Glancing over her shoulder, she saw the pockmarked face of a guard as he reached out for her. She yelped as he snatched her cloak. In a split second decision, Miriam unfastened the brooch. She fell forward, stumbling into a group of onlookers.

Gaining her feet, she met the eyes of two men she knew—one was a man who worked as hired muscle for a nearby inn, his neck the girth of her whole waist; the other was a dockhand and an equally bear-sized man. As men well accustomed to their share of scuffles, they quickly took in the situation. The dockhand stretched his trunk-thick neck and rolled his mighty shoulders, "You go now, missy, and don't run into any more trouble. We've got this for you." The two gave dark grins and without question created a barrier between her and the approaching guard.

With no time to thank her saviors, Miriam rose and tore through the crowd. Twice she glanced over her shoulder through the thicket of townspeople. More fireworks rattled the air and showered the streets in color. Through the chaos, she caught glimpses of the two men—her saviors—manhandling the guards like small toys. Yet the stream of guards was relentless, and for every man they took down, two more replaced them. Miriam turned the corner. She prayed for their safety as she ran home as quickly as she could, hoping against hope she wasn't too late.

Breathlessly, she burst through the door and took in the scene.

Two women stood in scarlet robes on the far side of the room beside the fireplace.Between the two, a man sat in a high-backed chair with his legs crossed—her father's favorite seat.He had the same scarlet robes, only his had a flaring collar with black trim.The black flame of the Citadel was emblazoned upon their breasts.*Three Reavers,* Miriam thought in awe.*Wait... why would three Reavers attend a simple Testing? Well, this wasn't a normal testing due to my age, so perhaps that's why... But still, why would my age warrant two more Reavers?* Her mind struggled to stay present, to think rationally when the sheer presence of those before her made her knees tremble. *Perhaps it's simply an honor,* her mind concluded. *No need to be so dramatic, Miriam,* she told herself and smiled, the matter settled.

She quickly examinedtheir stripes, denoting their rank. The woman on the left, with curly hair and an ample bosom, had one stripe. The blonde with fiery green eyes and a pompous tilt to her narrow face bore two stripes on her cuff. Miriam's eyes drifted back to the man in the chair. He was broad-shouldered with raven hair and slanted eyes like a snake. She eyed his stripes and nearly gasped. Four. The man was just short of the rank of Arbiter—though it was said that difference was the span of chasms. Each stripe took decades to achieve, and each was harder than the last. In the long lifetime of a Reaver, only few ever achieved their third stripe. That he bore the fourth stripe said this man was clearly not one to be reckoned with. *Odd again,* her mind whispered, but once more she reminded herself of the rarity of this occasion. Never had a girl been tested so old.

She then saw her father. He was a tall man with a thick gray mustache and sinewy arms from a life of hard trade. He rushed to her side. "Miriam! We've been waiting for you," he said, gripping her shoulders. "Are you all right?"

"I am now," she said, touching his arm in assurance.

"That's good." He breathed a sigh of relief. "I was worried you were hurt or worse. It seemed the only logical answer. I assured our dear Reaver Logan that you would not miss this moment even if you were strapped in chains." She tried to hide how close to the truth that was.

"Where in the world have you been?" her mother asked sharply.

Miriam turned to see her mother standing in the corner wearing her familiar blue silk dress. She was a beautiful woman, with bright eyes, and shiny flaxen hair that fell around her slender shoulders—she was far more feminine than Miriam ever was. Looking at her, she appeared a different breed of woman, or at least too different to be called her mother. She stood with arms crossed beneath her breasts looking generally uncomfortable with the whole situation. She flashed glances to a man in the corner who Miriam had not noticed. He was a short man, but it did not detract from his menace in the least for she saw his gray cloak with two-crossed swords. The cloak of a Devari. They were the guardians of the Citadel and wardens of the Reavers, the most elite of warriors. They had special powers of their own, derived from a source she had always been curious about called the Ki. Her mother eyed the man as if he was seconds from jumping out and biting her.

She remembered her mother had asked a question. "I got caught up," she said simply.

"And where's your brooch and cloak?" her mother asked, squinting.

Miriam gripped her chest where the brooch had been, suddenly remembering how she lost it. She struggled to come up with a lie, looking around the room. "I lost it in the marketplace," she said at last. "I think it must have been filched." She winced inwardly.

"How could it have been filched if it was upon your breast?" her mother asked.

"I took my cloak off to wrap the bread and wine. That's when it was stolen I think," she explained hurriedly.

Her mother nodded slowly. Her father seemed more cautious, but he kept it concealed. "Wait," her mother said, never the sharpest sword, "then where is the bread and wine for our guests?"

Miriam by now had time to construct a follow up lie, knowing this was an obvious flaw in her story. "I lost them as well. There was chaos in the commons' district. Some idiot let off a bunch of fireworks and I nearly got trampled. Honestly, mother, you should just be grateful I'm alive and standing here." She hoped her pluck wasn't too much, but the lie came

14

across smooth—well, she supposed it was actually the truth, if a tad construed. She never realized the truth could be such an easy alibi.

The two female Reaver's snorted as if twins.

"Spirited, isn't she?" said one.

They stood beside Logan like small fires before a raging hearth. Only her father's eyes narrowed at her lie, though the Devari's gaze made her skin clammy—*was it true as the rumors say that Devari were masters of deciphering fact from fiction?* She swallowed and tried to remove all emotion from her face.

"You can settle these petty family disputes later," Reaver Logan said at last. "Let us begin with the trial, that is, unless you have changed your mind, and you do not want to become a Reaver. Is this the case?"

"Nothing could be further from the truth. I am ready," she said with her back straight, returning his gaze. It was difficult, for the man's eyes seemed to bore through her.

"So be it," he said.

The other two women Reavers strode forward and gripped Miriam's shoulders. Her knees twitched, buckling beneath her. One of them had summoned the element of flesh, sparking her nerve, she realized. She accepted it, kneeling with head bent. Her heart raced. Miriam had heard the stories; she knew she had to remain still.

Logan approached, his steps sounding loud in her ears. He touched the side of her head.

Miriam held her breath and closed her eyes. She tried to summon the spark inside her, to show it like a guiding light so the man would be in awe of the power inside her. Her breath swelled with pride and hope, making her so light and dizzy she thought she would float into the air or faint. After what felt like an eternity, the man straightened. She smiled and opened her mouth, but Logan's brows drew down darkly.

"The Testing is over. Miriam, age fourteen, has failed to summon the spark," he declared.

Miriam felt her heart drop into the pit of her stomach. Bile stung her throat; she was going to be sick. *It's over... How is that possible?* She gazed down at her open palm. Even now, she felt the spark roiling inside her.

She looked up and into the Reaver's face. The man pulled on his snug leather gloves. He wore an expression of sympathy. It reminded her of one of her dolls as a child, painted bright blue eyes staring out woodenly. Everything about it was fake.

"No," she said, shaking her head, "you're lying."

The man said nothing as he motioned to the others, turning to depart.

Like a tidal wave, anger replaced her sorrow. She rose, shrugging off the two Reavers and striding forward.

"Miriam!" her mother shouted, moving to restrain her, but Miriam was too fast.

In her fit of rage, she saw a jagged fragment from a broken pot and snatched it from the ground. Raising it threateningly, she eyed Logan, holding his gaze. She saw in his eyes the gleam of power. The gleam of the spark she knew she had. "You lie," she said harshly. "Tell me the truth."

Logan smirked. "The truth? The truth is you are weak. There is no more truth than that. You hold a pittance of the spark, enough to rank below even the servants. Is that the truth you wanted to hear? Do you know how many young girls just like you I've had to tell the same thing? Do you think you are the only one with a dream? Why do you think every Reaver is so revered and feared? It's simple. Only the unique few are chosen for such a path. You, I can tell, have neither the strength of the spark, nor the strength of will to survive the hardships of training. In short, you are not worthy." His sympathetic eyes took a dark gleam, and he asked, almost sweetly, "That wasn't the truth you were expecting, was it?"

Miriam shook her head, angrily, if only to clear the tears away. She refused to believe his lies. "Tell me then, how come I can feel it welling inside me, even as we speak?" He was silent. "Answer me!" she screamed.

"Miriam!" her mother said, shocked. "What has gotten into you?"

She saw her father in the corner of her vision. He eyed her, compassion in his eyes. "Miriam, your mother is right this time. Let it go. He has no reason to lie. Sometimes it is the lies within ourselves that we must face."

"Father," she whispered, as tears leaked down her cheeks. This time something told her that even he was wrong. But she couldn't explain it. She feared any words she gave voice to would only prove her lunacy.

Towering head and shoulders over her, the Reaver spoke, drawing her attention back. He gazed down his sharp nose at her. "What exactly do you want, girl? Tell me so we can be done with this farce."

"I have the spark. I know it. Just as you do. Teach me to use it, that's all I ask. I will not disappoint."

"You ... are like me?"

Miriam held her ground. "If you give me a chance, I can be."

"Let's entertain this fantasy. Say we did teach you, what then? What use would you be? Years of the Citadel's valuable resources and time spent just so you could... what? Warm a tea kettle?"

Miriam felt her hand twitch, begging to smash the man's arrogant jaw, when the Devari spoke suddenly.

"There is no need to taunt the girl, Logan. There is an easy solution to all this." The man strode to the nearby table. He snatched a candle from the polished oak and returned.

"Light it," he ordered. "If she can, she has proven you wrong, Logan. If not, her own action should prove the harsh truth."

"A candle is nothing," Logan snapped. "Yet she cannot even do that. If it will end this pitiful squabbling, so be it."

Miriam looked to her mother and father. They watched her expectantly, hopefully. She looked back to the Devari. His steel-gray eyes were unreadable, but something in them made her feel as if he was rooting for her—perhaps for no other reason than to prove his arrogant counterpart wrong. Yet all thoughts fled as she stared at the long wick.

She gave a deep breath and delved inside. The tension in the air mounted. The spark wouldn't come. She wormed deeper into her mind, but it was as if she reached her hand into a brimming well only to find dry sand between her fingers. At last she dropped the sharp clay and fell to her knees. The Devari put the unlit candle back upon the table.

"We're done here," Logan said to his companions, turning to leave.

Miriam had trouble catching her breath. She tried to speak, but her voice was robbed from her throat. No, she fumed, she wouldn't cry, she couldn't show weakness in front of these people, least of all in front of this man! Yet even as she thought the words, she felt more hot tears cloud her vision. All her life she had waited for this moment, and this was her answer. She felt an arm encircle her shoulders and she saw her father's well-worn look of compassion.

Distantly, she saw Logan reach the door.

"Wait," her mother said, racing forward. "Aren't you forgetting something?"

"Such as?" Logan gave a strange smile.

Her mother cleared her throat awkwardly. Her father watched the exchange in confusion.

"Well... At least isn't there a reward? For the test, I mean. The family is given compensation for their beloved child? Five gold *lenars*, correct?"

"Seria! Can't you think about your daughter just this once?" her father said.

The Reaver scoffed, loud enough to silence both of them. "The Citadel should charge for every failed attempt as this is a waste of my valuable time, but luckily for you, the Patriarch is infinitely gracious. However, only if the child is deemed worthy does the family get compensated for their child's *services* for the Citadel. Your daughter is not worthy."

"But..." her mother blabbered, "You... I was promised! What about for...
"

"For?" Logan questioned, as if egging her mother on.

Her mother's mouth worked silently, and Miriam looked up in confusion, watching the exchange despite feeling drained of all life. At last her mother turned silent, lips pressing together in a thin, pale line. Logan's smile widened. The exchange baffled Miriam, but she no longer cared as

Logan turned, leaving. His hand paused upon the door. Miriam couldn't see his face, but somehow she could tell the man was smiling, still.

"You've heard the whispers, surely, have you not?" Logan asked without turning. "Fearful rumors that set the cowardly on edge..." The door was half-open and his frame was silhouetted by the dying purple and orange light of twilight.

Miriam of course knew what he was talking about. They all did. The Ronin—legendary warriors from an ancient age thought to have nearly caused the destruction of the world, now rumored to walk the lands once again. It was the talk of the town. Miriam had heard stories of the Ronin since she was a little girl. She knew them better than anyone. However, she was altogether different when it came to the legends told. Where every other father would tell stories of the Ronins' evil, her father told her stories of the Ronins' courage and might. To her, the Ronin were the greatest heroes who had ever lived. In truth, the only thing Miriam wanted more than becoming a Reaver was to be a Ronin. Yet she had always kept her father's stories secret. He had made her vow that she would never utter a word. Now the rumors of their return had made them all the more cautious, for a simple mention of their name was a crime punishable by death.

"We've all heard the rumors," her father said.

"What have you heard exactly?" Logan plied.

"That they have returned, or so the fools whisper."

Logan turned around, rising to his full height. "Yes. Fascinating tales, aren't they?"

Please father—keep quiet, she prayed. She feared he would praise the Ronin, the legends he held so highly. The veneration in his voice in every tale was too palpable to make her think otherwise.

At last, he spoke. "Yes, stories. That is all."

She gave a sigh of relief.

Logan narrowed his gaze as if he had been searching for a different answer. "The Return," he said sharply, as if trying to startle or shock those nearest. And it worked. The two women who wore masks of serenity flinched at the name, shifting their feet nervously. Even the Devari looked away, as if the mere mention of the infamous Return was too much to bear. Logan continued. "The evil that plagued the lands two millennium ago has returned, or so they say. Perhaps this time it is more than stories."

"Only a child or a fool would think so," her father said, clearly implying the latter. "And of course, you are neither. Why do you still bother us with these questions? You have tested our daughter, and she has proved unworthy in your eyes. Leave us in peace!"

Logan's head cocked to the side, his raven hair spilling across his shoulders. He slowly circled her father like a bird of prey as he spoke. "Oh, I will. Trust me, I want nothing more than to flee this hovel," he said as he picked up a dull red apple from the nearby table. Eyeing her father, his upper lip curled as he dropped it, grinding the fruit beneath his heel into a juicy pulp. "Yet, there is another reason we are here."

"What do you mean?" Miriam asked.

Logan ignored her, still speaking to her father. "It is the reason your precious daughter was tested when no other girl after the age of ten is ever tested. Did you ever question that? She is beyond the Age of Initiation, and yet here we are."

Miriam spoke again, stepping forward, "I have the spark ... Why else would you be here?" Her heart began to race.

"The truth is we've heard that there are those who have said their name. In fact, the claim is far bolder, that benevolent words have been shed for those we do not name. That they have even spewed lies about *their* courage! Could you imagine such blasphemy?"

"Enough with your foul insinuations! Who would spread such blatant vitriol?" her father said.

Logan smirked. "Really, does it matter? Know only that it is a valid source."

"And how would I know that? You could be making this up for all I know!"

"I am not," he said flatly, picking at his nails, "I have far better things to do than to question the likes of you. Yet, alas, your crime is most heinous, and those in power wanted it seen to in the most efficient and expedient manner possible. Thus, my presence." He said with a mock bow, his dark red cloak fanning to both sides.

"Answer me! Who told you those lies?" her father shouted.

Logan nodded to one Reaver and the Devari. The Devari had a sickly look upon his stony face. It sent a shiver down Miriam's spine. The Reaver with two stripes approached.

"Father, run!" she shouted.

Suddenly the door slammed shut by an invisible hand.

The female Reaver knocked her father to his knees, clubbing him with an invisible force.

"Let him go!" Miriam shrieked, running towards her father.

She felt a blow to the back of her head and stumbled to her knees. When she looked up, the Reaver with one stripe clenched her hair painfully with one fist. "It's time for you to be quiet now and watch," the woman hissed.

Suddenly Miriam gagged as a collar pressed around her neck. Her fingertips groped at a ring of steel.

Logan slowly approached her father, towering over him as he knelt, dazed. "Speak their name."

"No," her father said. "Tell me who told you, and let me go or so help me—"

"I don't believe you are in the position to make threats," said Logan, "and I'm afraid I can't do either of those things. The truth is you will die for your crimes, so why do you care who it was? It matters not."

"Who told you?" Her father's voice was stone.

Logan sighed. "Your persistence is somehow admirable. Fine, I care not. Your feared betrayer is closer than you'd ever think." His eyes flashed to the corner of the room, if only for an instant, but it was as clear as if he had shouted it.

Her mother swallowed, backed against the wall as if she knew this moment was coming. Her fair hair was plastered to the sides of her face as sweat ran down her once-pretty features.

"Why?" her father whispered, his voice hoarse. He winced, hand gripping his heart as if it were splintering inside his chest. He tried to speak again but only a pained groan escaped his lips.

Her mother opened her mouth, but nothing came out.

Logan threw up his hands, "I'll save you both the time and tell you. Money. Isn't it always such petty trifles with you ungifted? Now, I have a final offer for you so we can end this pathetic charade. Speak their name aloud, and I will contemplate sparing you," he said, and then raised a single finger. "But if you do not, you will surely die. Renounce them, curse them, anything but the lies you have been spouting, and I will consider your salvation."

Miriam felt tears flowing down her face. "Say their name, father," she pleaded. "Please. Curse them. I will say it if you do not."

He looked to her, and shook his head.

Miriam saw and understood that look. It was the look of resolute acceptance, and she wanted with every ounce of her being to exchange places. She closed her eyes, and quickly summoned her spark. There was nothing there, as if it was gone entirely.

When she opened her eyes, her father looked up, head held high, and spoke. "The Ronin are coming."

"A decent start. Continue. Tell me of their cruelty and foul nature or—"

Her father interrupted Logan, his voice gaining strength and filling the room with its conviction, "Consider this your fortune. You, Reaver, will die a pathetic coward at the hands of a Ronin's blade." Logan twitched in anger, opening his mouth, but he was cut off again. "You will never escape their justice, no matter what dark gods you pray to, or what dirty hovel you attempt to hide in, you will always be weak and always living in fear until they find you and end your miserable life. They will burn every wicked fool to the ground who thinks that they hold the faintest candle to the heroes of Farhaven."

Logan's whole body shook with rage upon each successive word. With a single breath he closed his eyes and extended his hand. Her father suddenly burst into flames. Miriam gasped, every muscle in her body froze.

In place of her father was a spray of blood, skin, and bone on the wood floor. With another flash of fire, the pile turned to ash.

"Well, that was most unpleasant," Logan said with a breath, flicking a spot of blood from his cheek. "As I said, that is a name punishable by death. And coupled with the fact that you yourself assaulted a Reaver, another crime punishable by death, you all can consider yourselves lucky that only one of you had to pay the price." The man turned to leave. The Reaver who was holding Miriam let her go, and the metal shackle around her neck shattered.

Horror and confusion warred inside her as she tried to find words, but only a choking sound escaped her lips. She stumbled, falling to her knees where her father's tall form had been. Her fingers sifted through the bloody ash, disbelieving.Rage and pain swirled inside her like a storm. She heard her mother's wails distantly. She ignored them. Her eyes fixed on the tall man before her. The man she had wanted to become. The scarlet red robes were now blurred as tears of rage welled in her eyes. She rose to her feet, channeling every ounce of life and power within her.

"She's threading," one of the Reavers said, backing away. She saw them form swirling balls of earth in their hands, readying themselves. Yet Miriam saw a curious gleam in their eyes.

Fear.

"I can sense it," replied the vile man, his tone all arrogance. "So it seems you can thread the elements. Curious why I couldn't see it until now, unless..." His eyes widened, "It must be. You are one of those Untamed whose latent abilities only surface under duress. A shame. What a useless waste of the gift. Kill her," he said with a careless wave.

Before either Reaver could move, Miriam cried out. She flung her arms to either side, fire erupting from her palms. Both Reavers reacted, erecting thick barriers of earth. Yet the Reaver of one stripe was too slow. Fire engulfed her spell. Like tinder sparked by flint, she exploded in flames. In a flash the fire disappeared, leaving nothing behind but a small amount of smoldering ash.

Logan gave a thin, fox-like smile. "Ah, vengeance. How does it taste? I killed one of yours, now you killed one of mine. Are you satisfied?"

"I've barely begun," Miriam seethed and the torrent of fire that pressed against the woman's shield grew. The fire singed the cuffs of her two stripes and she cried out.

"Logan! Save me! Kill the fool girl!"

The man twitched as the fire grew—it was clear he cared more for this woman. Miriam felt vengeance flash hot inside her, but then Logan's face turned smooth. "A Reaver would never fall to such a pathetic being. It will only prove that you are not truly worthy to wear the scarlet robes."

At his words, Miriam let the fire grow. She felt the woman thread filaments of water, hoping to dampen the effect of the raging flames. It merely fueled Miriam's anger, and she fought back with more fire. With her cry pitching, she whipped her arm like a cord and a ball of fire shot out. The Reaver shrieked. An explosion of flames snuffed her cries.

Distantly, Miriam saw her mother cowering in the corner. The terror in her mother's bright blue eyes was evident, as if she gazed upon a monster. Miriam only smirked. *Let her watch what her greed has bought her.*

A slow clap drew her attention forward to the man she truly wanted dead.

The Devari who had remained remarkably silent, spoke abruptly. "Let go of the anger, girl. You do not want to become him. Trust me."

Logan laughed. "And what is so wrong with me, Devari? Giving into our passions and desires fully is what grants us our most potent wishes. In truth, it's what makes us human. Your emotions, on the other hand, remain restrained behind that wall of yours. You will never understand. This girl might still have potential. If she wasn't an Untamed, I would consider using her as my apprentice." He turned to Miriam with a lustful gleam in his eyes. "Would you like that? I shall contemplate it, but only if you beg me right here and now upon your knees."

Memory of her father being seared to ash and blood flashed before her eyes. Her rage conquered all other thoughts. "You … killed … him…"

Without a word, she raised both arms and a flash of livid fire shot forth. Logan erected a swift barrier of steel, but she wasn't done. She cried out and the fire grew until it engulfed the man completely. Heat singed her face as nearby chairs exploded, and curtains disintegrated. She heard faint screams but they were muffled beneath her rage. *Let it all burn,* her mind seethed, watching as the bloody ash upon the ground where her father had been was incinerated by the firestorm. Her body shook with power, barely able to withstand the torrent flooding through her. At last, when she could withstand it no longer, she let her arms fall. In a sudden flash, the fire winked out of existence. Miriam sagged, falling to her knees. Every muscle in her body ached. She sucked in a ragged breath, pushing herself up. She watched the smoke clear from where Logan had stood.

Nothing.

Suddenly, a dark form unfurled. Logan stood straight. A steel skin sluiced off his dark robes like silver water and his upper lip curled as he stared at Miriam. "I didn't think I'd have to use that. Were I anything less than a fourth stripe, I would be dead. There are those who have attained the third stripe with only half your power. Yet, sadly for you, the gap between three and four stripes is an abyss you cannot possibly comprehend."

Shakily, Miriam summoned her tired muscles, forcing herself to rise. *He doesn't know I don't have more inside me. Stand!* her stubborn mind shouted, locking her legs at last.

"There's no use," Logan said, as if reading her thoughts, "you can barely lift a finger. It's obvious. You've used every last ounce of your spark. You must rest a full day in order to recover fully. If you attempt to thread anymore, you will likely die. It's an all too common occurrence among the untrained in the Citadel. In short, you have failed."

Logan paused. "Yet I have a proposition for you. It has been a very long time since anyone has made me summon that much of the spark. I see a glimmer of potential in you. If you still desire, I will train you to become a Reaver."

Miriam's heart clenched. The man gave a knowing smirk, as if he recognized her conflict at being proffered her dream from the man who had taken away everything.

He spoke before she could. "If it makes your decision any easier, there is also this to consider. As it stands, you will be charged with the murder of two Reavers. The only punishment for such a heinous crime is death by hanging. As a Reaver has never been killed within the walls of Farbs, it would be made public—a spectacle for all to see. And I would watch, as well, as the life faded from those pretty eyes."

"It was not my fault..." she found herself saying, falling to her knees.

"Ah, but even if it were not true, the word of a four stripe Reaver over that of a simple commoner? Who would they believe?"

Miriam shook her head, tears flowing down her cheeks. "You can't..." Yet she knew it to be the truth. There was no refuting the word of a Reaver, especially one of Logan's rank. She looked up into his eyes, hating him yet pleading for mercy. She clutched her neck, as if she could already feel the coarse rope of the noose tightening around it.

"But you must do one last thing, Miriam. You must kill her. She has seen and heard too much." Logan nodded to her mother who wept in the corner of the room in fear.

"No, please..." Her mother stumbled to form words.

The Devari spoke abruptly. "You've gone too far, Logan," he said gripping his twin blades.

"Stay out of this, Raemis!" Logan snapped, raising an arm to the man. Tendrils of fire danced before his fingertips. "Do not let your pride overcome your good sense, Devari."

Raemis growled, but made no move.

Miriam felt her body jostle. She looked down and saw her mother. The woman gripped the skirts of Miriam's singed dress with shaking hands.

"Miriam, dearest, listen to me, you can't do this," she stuttered. "Do you hear me?" Miriam refused to look down, to see those traitorous eyes. Her mother suddenly bellowed, "Miriam, I am your mother, look at me!"

With ice in her heart, she looked down upon the woman.

Her mother gasped. "Miriam..."

"You are not my mother," she said in a cold voice, brushing aside her hands. She knew what her mother looked upon were dead, pitiless eyes—there was no emotion left for the woman who cowered before her. It was suddenly clear to Miriam what had to be done. The woman before her was a dark stain, an abscess, and she could start anew by simply wiping the stain clean. For her father, for her own life, and for her dream ... a dream she had vowed to see through, no matter the obstacle. "This is compassion, mother."

Miriam raised her arm until she felt her mother's hot and fearful last breaths upon her outstretched palm.

"Yes!" Logan exclaimed. She could feel his grin spreading like grease upon her skin. "You are beginning to understand what must be done to become a Reaver. You must sacrifice all for the sake of the spark. Now end her pitiful life and let us leave this hovel and move to far grander heights. To the place you rightfully belong."

Miriam felt every muscle in her body wanting to seek vengeance for her father's death, knowing her mother was partly responsible. Her hand flexed, sending a tremor up her arm as she looked into those empty, pleading eyes. How could she possibly kill her own mother? Yet if she didn't, she would be killed. No, worse. Reavers were the peacekeepers of Farhaven and she had murdered two of them in cold blood. *If I don't do this, the entire world will loathe me. I'll be the furthest thing from a Ronin and from my father's heart. Everything that he held dear, I would destroy. My very death would stain his memory forever.*

The room shuddered as the door crashed open. A figure stood in the doorway.

Outside, Miriam noticed a familiar sight in the darkening night. It was the *lecarta* with its scarlet curtains and long carrying poles. Men and women stood just beyond the door, waiting patiently. She even spotted some of the guards from earlier including the pockmarked face of the guard who grabbed her. She looked back to the slender figure in the doorway whose small frame commanded her attention.

She was adorned in dark clothes, deep blues and greens only softened by a lavender *shaka* that hid all but wisps of her midnight hair. Those eyes... Miriam grew cold, feeling fear to her bones. The woman's gaze was like an amber fire that took her breath away.

Upon her entrance, Logan froze. She could see every muscle in his body turn to stone. At once, he shot to one knee and bowed deeply. "Peace and strength upon you, I live to serve," he quoted, a quick and fierce whisper.

"What is going on here, Logan?"

"Initiation, sister," he replied quickly.

"Ah, and is this how we initiate our brothers and sisters? By making them slaughter their own loved ones in cold blood?"

He fell to both knees, head scraping the bloody wood beneath him. "No, sister."

"Explain yourself. Quickly." Despite her simple words and soft voice, the threat of violence was unmistakable. Who was this woman who could command a four-stripe Reaver? Miriam wondered. She had neither stripes nor even scarlet robes.

"My deepest apologies, sister, I only meant to find the true merit of the girl and the depth of her conviction."

"I believe she has proven that," the woman said, eyeing Miriam whose hand still hovered over her mother's face.

The woman approached. Miriam tried to move, but she was rooted. She had trouble taking a breath in the presence of this woman, as if an aura of power was making her suffocate. Miriam stepped back and realized she wasn't imagining things. The very air was thicker around the woman. "I came when I sensed a powerful presence," she said, looking at Logan. "The whole Citadel should have felt the amount of spark that was channeled here. What am I to say to the Patriarch?"

"I—" Logan began.

The woman laughed, "I was not speaking to you, Logan." She let down her *shaka*. Miriam nearly gasped at her beauty. She had a diamond-shaped face with smooth olive skin and full lips that held a permanent inquisitive twist. She smiled suddenly, but her red lips held no warmth and it touched none of her flawlessly smooth features. "You have a great gift, child."

Miriam swallowed, nodding her head in thanks.

"Do you know who I am?"

She shook her head no.

"My name is Fera, but many know me by my title. I am an Arbiter."

Miriam's heart clenched in terror. An Arbiter... She thought they were only stories. There had only been three in all time—they lived for thousands of years, the strength of their spark giving them near immortality, or so it was said.

"Ar..." Miriam stuttered. She eyed the floor and moved to prostrate herself when Arbiter Fera stopped her.

"While many should, you have no need to fear me, child," she said and lifted her chin to look her in the eyes. Those eyes... "What is your name?" Arbiter Fera asked.

"Miriam," she breathed.

"A beautiful name for one with such a beautiful talent. You have no idea of the extent of your power, do you Miriam?"

Again, she shook her head, afraid to speak and let anything out that might offend this woman.

Arbiter Fera turned. "And you, Devari, what part have you played in this little escapade? The truth now."

Even Raemis seemed shaken by the woman's appearance. "I will not lie. I attempted to stop Logan when he wanted the mother dead. The girl has seen enough death this day."

"I see," Arbiter Fera said slowly. She turned, letting her blue and green robes whisk along the ground. With a snap of her fingers, suddenly the Devari shrieked. It was so loud and sharp that Miriam clapped her hands to her ears and shut her eyes. When she opened them, chainmail, a sword, and clothes clattered to the ground where Raemis had stood only a moment before.

"A shame," Arbiter Fera said with a sigh. "He was a dutiful man, but sadly we cannot have those who disagree with the decisions of a four stripe Reaver."

"Thank you, sister," Logan professed, "your words are a beacon of light to us all."

"I wasn't finished," Arbiter Fera said in a dark tone that made Miriam's blood run cold. Logan's face turned pale as the woman rounded, looming over him. "You are a reckless fool."

"I..." Logan stuttered, fumbling for his smooth words. "Sister, I apologize for my indiscretion, but you must understand—"

"—Silence!" she bellowed, her words a thunderclap that shook the walls. Logan's lips pressed tight. "Listen closely. If you ever attempt to use your power as you have done today, know I will do far worse than I have done to that man. You will beg for any sort of death but the one I will give you. Now promise me that we will never have this conversation again."

All blood drained from Logan's face. "I promise, sister," he said in a fearful murmur.

"Good," Arbiter Fera said with a smile and circled an arm around Miriam's shoulders. The woman was barely her height, yet she seemed to tower. She felt her body shake as the woman held her. "Now come, Miriam. Logan was right about one thing. This place is no longer your home." Miriam nodded softly. Clenching her eyes tightly, she allowed the Arbiter to blindly steer her past the chain and leather, between the charred corpses of the two Reavers, and over the spot of burnt ash where her father had knelt. Only when she felt the cold air of the night did she open her eyes, allowing the horrors she had seen to melt into a disorienting dream.

Outside, torches had been lit and two bare-chested, muscled men pulled back the curtains of the *lecarta*. Several others knelt, creating a path of human flesh to its entry. In the corner of her eye and over Arbiter Fera's arm, Miriam spotted two men. They were bloodied, bruised, and shackled. She recognized them—it was the dockhand and the bruiser.

"Wait," she said, summoning a tiny voice.

Arbiter Fera paused. "What is it, dear girl?"

"I..." She swallowed, hoping that exposing one truth wouldn't lead to the discovery of another. The last thing she wanted was for this woman with her piercing golden eyes to discover that Miriam was the one who started the skirmish in the marketplace. She chose her words carefully. "I know those two men. What is their judgment?"

"They are to be hanged upon the dawn."

She swallowed, finding her courage, "I don't know what they did, but they are good men. Could you perhaps find it in your heart to let them free?"

Arbiter Fera snorted softly—she somehow made it seem dignified. "My good child, these two good men killed three of my own and wounded many others. How could I justify such a thing to the people?"

"Surely someone in your position needs no justification," she replied softly.

"Ah, you are clever for your age, but not yet wise, my dear. True wisdom lies in not abusing one's authority. When I was your age, a captain of a vessel taught me a lesson. He said to me, 'A good sailor does not plow through shallow, rocky waters because he can, but instead he finds the deepest current. And only when all other options are exhausted does he take the shallow path.'"

Miriam nodded. She saw the wisdom; yet she could not in good conscience let these men die. She would see some justice prevail today. She held back her fear and spoke. "Then I believe this is one of those times. I will not go with you unless those two men are set free. And if they are, I promise you I will train hard every single day and make you proud of your choice." She readied herself, half-preparing to be incinerated to ash or evaporated like the Devari.

Her eyelids flickered as Arbiter Fera smiled softly. "You will be a force to be reckoned with one day, my dear Miriam. And may Selivas bless the man you choose to wed," she laughed. Miriam only half understood, but before she knew it, Arbiter Fera nodded to the men holding her friends and they were released from their shackles. Both men flashed her knowing smiles of gratitude and then turned, heading away quickly as if afraid someone would change their mind.

"Come now, girl, set your mind on the sights ahead." With that, Arbiter Fera offered her slender hand. Miriam took it and entered the *lecarta* when there was a loud explosion. She threw back the scarlet veil to see her home erupt in a torrent of flames, feeling the intense heat upon her face.

She turned to the woman next to her. Arbiter Fera merely smirked. "Time to leave all this behind us, Neophyte Miriam."

Miriam nodded in understanding, turning away so the woman couldn't see the tears leak down her face as the men lifted the *lecarta* and they were carried away, towards the great stone fortress in the distance.

Towards   her   dream.

r o n i n s a g a . c o m

Made in the USA
Middletown, DE
10 August 2020

14942035R00020